Swarm

a Novella

David Q. Hall

Printed in the United States of America
First Printing 2022
All rights reserved.

ISBN: 978-1-948894-32-6

Copyright © 2022 by David Q. Hall

Tree Shadow Press

www.treeshadowpress.com

DEDICATION

This novella is dedicated to a real-life Eric.

He was my colleague and best friend in the large office where I started my retirement career.

Along with his friendship, I will forever be indebted to him for his daily greeting to me when we would arrive to start a new workday about 6:00 am.

I would say "Eric, how are you today?"

He would flash his perennial smile and reply, "Every day above ground is a good day."

He was a good friend.

ACKNOWLEDGMENTS

Swarm comes, in part, from the years the author spent as a hobbyist beekeeper. His honeybee hives were delightful to tend, and the honey produced was prodigious and delicious. Very top grade. The bees taught him a lot.

Even more, the main character in the story, Professor Eric Darden, a retired teacher in college, is based on a number of African American men whom the author was privileged to have known, was friends with, and to whom he listened intensely, over many years. It is fervently hoped that the story expresses with humility and authenticity their lifelong struggles against an entrenched racism that has plagued American society since Jamestown in 1619.

The author has tried to offer a true representation of what those men told him personally.

CHAPTER ONE
The Deadly Race

Lance Jones and his perpetual sidekick, Steven "Skater" Kelly, literally ran for their lives. They ran and ran, down crumbling sidewalks, across pot-holed streets, through vacant lot "shortcuts." They had to escape.

They were good runners. Lance, about five foot ten and 160 pounds, had been a quarter-miler on his old Flint Northern High School track squad. Skater was shorter and lighter. He had been Lance's teammate, specializing in longer distance. Neither one could outrun their threat.

Their pain, swelling, redness and itching increased block by block. But the rapid progression of their skin discomfort wasn't even noticeable compared to the headaches, the dizziness, the nausea and vomiting. After about half a mile of running that gradually slowed and became staggering and off-balance, the two friends each felt ready to pass out and collapse.

They probably would have done so, right where they were on the street, but now they were within sight of their gang "headquarters." The old, mostly abandoned, office building spurred both of them to make an extra effort to get to its familiar safety. With blurred vision and shaky legs, they bolted inside. It was more than they could manage to climb the stairs up to their second-floor gang "office." Skater lunged for an old lounge sofa in the lobby and collapsed there. Lance didn't make it quite that far. He collapsed into a twitching, convulsing heap on the floor just inside the inner door of the entrance.

Fellow members of the North Side Viking Raiders looked aghast and confused at the sight of the two. Their faces were so reddened and swollen that they were scarcely recognizable. One gang member said, "Somebody call 'Doc.'"

"Doc" was a former medic in the Marine Corps who regularly treated and stitched up their cuts from things like knife fights. Once he had probed and removed a lead bullet from a member's arm after a shooting.

"No, this is more serious," another gang member countered. "Let's take them to the emergency room at Hamilton."

Nobody was about to call 911. They never encouraged police, fire, ambulances, or any other public officials to "visit" their headquarters. The Viking Raiders had squatted at the old McLaren office building for a number of years now, and they tried to remain as low-profile as possible.

But in the end result, neither "Doc," or Hamilton Health Center, or emergency services of any kind, were needed. Lance died of severe anaphylactic shock and poisoning where he continued to lie on the lobby floor. Skater followed him into eternity only minutes later.

There was no particular reason to suspect that it was murder.

CHAPTER TWO

Professor Eric Darden, Retired

Eric Darden was unusual as a college professor. When he had started his college education in 1962, the private university in which he had enrolled was named General Motors Institute of Technology. It was located not far from the eventually infamous Flint River. "GMI," as it was known, had only been awarding bachelor's degrees to students for about sixteen years. There were only a limited number of African American students in an undergraduate population of around two thousand. There were no African American professors on the faculty.

But GMI had turned out to be a good choice for Eric. As long as he could find a GM division to sponsor his application, and he had an outstanding academic record in high school, their co-op program made it possible for him to get a college education. It was an unusual way of "working one's way through school."

GMI had sometimes been referred to as "the West Point of the Automotive Industry." Their primary mission was to create business and industry leaders by means of their co-op model. School, beginning with freshman level manufacturing courses, and work in GM facilities, were mixed in six-week rotations. Half of their student body at any given time would be attending their courses in classrooms. The other half would be out in GM manufacturing plants, earning the money they needed. Since the corporate mission was to train the engineers and executives GM needed, tuition was also partly subsidized.

Eric could not have afforded his college education had it not been for the GMI model. He managed to graduate after his fifth year near the top of his class. To support him and his value to GM, the corporation had gone so far as to sponsor his admission to graduate school also. He applied and was accepted to Michigan State University in their Psychology Department. He was further backed by a General Motors Scholarship. Without it more advanced education would not have been within his means.

His area of study was in the psychology of creating satisfied and productive workers in manufacturing. His dissertation to complete his doctoral program and degree had been entitled, "Psychological Elements Essential to the Most Productive Members of the Work Force." With a slightly altered title and a less heavily academic bent, it was published by GM as a training handbook for not only all of its GMI students, but all of their worldwide corporate executives.

It came to the surprise of probably only Eric himself that he was hired as an assistant professor by GMI after he graduated his doctoral program in 1977. He was the first African American member of the faculty. General Motors had taken him in, provided for him, gave him a professional "home," and the promise of a lifelong career.

There had been costs, however, to Eric in this nurturing environment. At one point when he was on a production line in the Flint Truck Assembly plant, he suffered a crippling accident. Part of his work training experience was to observe first-hand production and assembly lines. A union line worker lost his grip on a heavy tray of parts and it fell on Eric's left foot. Most of the bones in that foot were crushed.

It was an unfortunate error. The tray should never have been transferred from the cart without at least two workers handling it. Eric had been stretchered out of the line and taken to McLaren

Flint Hospital. A series of surgeries that year corrected and rebuilt as much of the damaged foot as medically possible. Months in a wheelchair, with a walker, eventually a cane, all accompanied by intensive physical therapy, helped with his rehabilitation.

But Eric being Eric, he somehow managed to keep up with his schoolwork and graduated on time. He also worked as diligently as humanly possible on his recovery. Years later, however, he still had to use the cane and walked with a pronounced limp. He never let the experience throw him off-course in his ambitions and work. Off-balance in his gait, yes, but not off of his dreams and goals. He was committed.

He did well as an assistant professor at GMI. By 1981, not knowing that a General Motors task force had recommended the company drop the institute within two years, Eric had become one of the most appreciated and best liked professors by the dwindling student body. They saw the upbeat and encouraging psychology professor as someone who helped them become productive managers of personnel.

The university's name was formally changed to Kettering University in 1998. Eric had been kept on the faculty at that point for over 21 years. He was entitled to a company pension upon retirement. By then in his mid-fifties, with his lingering physical limitations and his personal circumstances, he decided to take early retirement and not make the transition to Kettering and its different mission and programs.

Although there were some years ahead before GM would decide to get out of "the pension business," the trend was already happening. Corporate "bean counters" convinced the genial professor that a lump-sum buyout would be more to his benefit than a small payout in an annuity from the pension fund. He accepted their offer. An early retirement at close to 55 meant that he would have to wait several years before he could draw federal Social Security benefits. He needed the cash in his transition. The royalties from his widely used book and other professional articles always went to GM. They were legally "work product," and belonged to the corporation.

CHAPTER THREE
Eric Darden, the Man

Eric had a tough childhood. His family were longtime residents of the Flint North Side, where the majority of the population was African American in ancestry and identity. His father was one of the thousands of workers on the assembly line in that same Flint truck plant where Eric was injured many years later. His mother was a secretary in the Supervisor's office at the plant. An older sister and older brother had been expelled from the family home on the North Side as soon as they each turned eighteen.

"Time you supported yourselves," his dad had barked. "Stop leaching offa me."

That left only his mom and himself to be the recipient of Dad's drunken outbursts of rage and violence. Too many late clock-ins, too many missed days on the assembly line, and too many senseless fights with co-workers eventually resulted in Dad losing his job at the truck plant. Loss of job meant loss of regular paycheck, but more alcohol and violent outbursts at home. Or at the bar. Or in the lockup. And eventually in the prison yard at Ionia Correctional Facility. He died of cirrhosis of his liver while incarcerated. There had been no way to cure, or even reverse, the liver damage.

The elimination of alcohol consumption in prison in no way stopped or reduced his addiction to violent behavior. He was undiagnosed and untreated for an alcohol-related disorder expressed in multiple aggressive behaviors. Dante Darden exhibited most of the signs and symptoms of "intermittent explosive disorder" (IED). He was physically aggressive. He was verbally aggressive and abusive. He was prone to angry outbursts, often with no apparent cause. He physically attacked family, co-workers, bar patrons, sometimes even complete strangers. And he damaged property and objects without restraint

Eric's mom, Florence, did her best to shield her children from much of Dante's violent outbursts and physical blows. She took the brunt of it herself. There were innumerable painful visits to urgent care and hospital emergency rooms as a result. The cracked ribs, the broken eye socket, the dislocated joints, a lost tooth and much bruising and bleeding were unmistakable to many medical care providers. The excuses offered were all too typical.

"I fell down the stairs. I'm so clumsy."

"I walked right into a door. I have to look where I'm going."

"I smacked myself with my own mop. So much for hard scrubbing."

"I had too much to drink. Fell headfirst into the kitchen counter." Flo didn't drink. She couldn't after seeing the effect on her alcoholic husband.

On many occasions she had winced in pain after Dante's blows as he stormed out to make things worse at his favorite bar. She would talk to her children, especially Eric, the youngest.

"You know, your father doesn't mean what he says and does. He loves you, but he doesn't know how to show it. He's sick. He'll get better. Things will be better. You have to believe. Love is stronger than hate. Good is stronger than evil. God and his angels will protect you. You have to be strong and not let the bad defeat you. Fear shall be overcome by your bravery. Be determined and you will win in the end."

Young Eric Darden had absorbed his mother's teaching like a

man dying of thirst in a baking desert. He drank of her words like they were his only hope and salvation. An exceptionally bright and able student, he applied himself to his study and schoolwork like a drowning man clinging to a life preserver. His father had not thought much of his "book learning."

"You don't need all of those damn books to work on the line," he raged more than once. "You tellin' me what I do for you ain't good enough?" *Whack.* "There, you like that better?"

One time he drunkenly grabbed Eric's textbook and threw it into the outside trash can. Eric sobbed as his mother went out to retrieve it. But only after Dante had gone to the basement refrigerator for another sixpack.

"You never mind," she whispered to Eric. "You keep studying and earning good grades, and you'll be successful. A good education will be your ticket to a good future. A better life than this."

Eric the college professor remembered his mother's dying words as though they were last treasures from the Truth of God Himself.

"I'm so proud of you, my son! You made it. Always hold your head up high. You showed 'em all. Never let them defeat you. Smile when you think of me, 'cause I'll always be looking down at you."

Florence Darden's passing in 1989 was a loss Eric never quite got over. But he couldn't let it, or anyone, defeat him. Momma said that.

His momma also always told him to "keep happy thoughts in your head, and a smile on your face."

"Any problem you encounter in life is not The Problem. The problem is how you think and act about it. If there's a problem, it's in your attitude and your 'stinkin' thinking.'" She didn't have to give him context for Eric to recognize the Al-Anon reference. "So, you better think positive and act hopefully. It'll all work out." So that's what Eric did his entire life.

CHAPTER FOUR
Eric's Soulmate

Eric kept a disciplined schedule and unrelenting, strenuous effort to rehabilitate from his foot-crushing accident. It was in the physical therapy unit at McLaren Clinic that he met the therapist who helped him "work it all out." Her name was Mary. Their relationship at first was thoroughly professional and case related. She appropriately saw him and treated him as another patient. He respected her knowledge, skill, and conscientious work at physical rehabilitation. But over time they "connected."

It took literally months, but Eric fell in love with this beautiful young woman who emerged as the most caring, helpful, tender, positive person he had ever met in his life. His mother excepted. Mary McCormick had appropriately and professionally "compartmentalized" her initial attraction to him and suppressed it. But over time she also fell in love with the most decent, kind, thoughtful, positive person *she* had ever met.

After months of work together on helping him regain the ability to stand, walk, and maintain steady balance using that damaged left foot, it was she who worked up the courage to ask him to join her for a lunch break.

"Oh, thank God and praise the Lord," Eric couldn't help from blurting out. "I was trying to muster the courage to invite *you* to do the same thing." Mary didn't mind the religious expression. She was a lifelong Baptist, and when she learned incidentally that Eric was African Methodist Episcopal (AME), she surprised herself by immediately thinking, *Close enough.* A common religious faith was only one of the many, many things in common that emerged as they got to know each other.

That first lunch was one of many that followed. Finally, there was a romantic dinner out at an over-priced, but very nice, restaurant in downtown Flint. There were a few movies, no sports events since neither of them was especially "into" sports. But only slightly to each other's surprise, they really enjoyed going to an occasional concert by the Flint Symphony Orchestra at the Flint Institute of Music. They also enjoyed the Flint Youth Symphony Orchestra. And it was not only the music. Both delighted in the budding talents of young people. Feeling a little corny and affectionate after one event, Eric smiled and said,

"You know, you and I really harmonize well together."

"Oh, sugar," Mary smiled back and did a little alluring eye flutter, "and in more ways than one." Eric *really* liked that.

At first, the goodnight kiss was restrained, polite, mildly affectionate. The spark of attraction and passion ignited, however. Their falling in love built up momentum as they spent time together. Without the need to put it into words, particularly early on, they each knew that they had found their soulmate.

Mary was an only child whose parents had both died in a tragic auto accident when she was only five. She had been raised by a grandmother who was deceased by the time she met Eric. For all practical purposes she had no family of her own. That void was more than filled by falling in love with Eric. They were married shortly after Eric graduated from the old GMI, the summer before he started at Michigan State University for his doctoral program in 1972. Mary went with him to East Lansing, where she found a good physical therapy clinic to work at and support the two while Eric studied and researched.

They were a good match, perfect partners for each other. She almost worshiped Eric's relentless determination, work ethic, and his insistence on being upbeat and looking always for the positive. She especially respected his outstanding intelligence and psychological insights into human behavior. Eric, on the other hand, thought that Mary was the most wonderful woman who ever walked the face of the earth. She even surpassed his sainted mother. He had the utmost respect for her professional knowledge and skill. She had done wonders in helping Eric recover his ability to stand and walk again. And it was obvious she also did her utmost to aid healing and recovery for all of her other patients and clients. Anyone looking up "mutual admiration society" would surely have found a photo of the two of them.

They tried, but had no children of their own. They discussed the common alternatives for childless couples who loved kids. They looked at fostering, at adoption, even at providing temporary sheltering for kids in transition in the Child Protective Services system. But nothing seemed to work out. Eric's strenuous efforts to complete his doctorate. Mary's demanding work schedule. Then Eric's search for a college teaching position. Then Mary's having to enable their moving locations several times...well, life just got complicated and "in the way."

And then, when Eric got established and had a regular teaching schedule at his old General Motors Institute, came Mary's shocking diagnosis of ovarian cancer. It is the cancer commonly referred to as "the cancer that whispers," because the great majority of women do not experience symptoms until it is in terribly late stages. Once diagnosed, it is difficult to treat. They tried everything possible with Mary – surgery, chemotherapy, radiation, homeopathic medicines and remedies – but nothing worked. Unusual for a woman as young as she was, merely fifty, Mary died of the ovarian cancer in 2000.

The entire experience wiped out every resource and asset the soulmates could scrape together. It exhausted insurance coverage. It completely drained meager savings. It maxed out credit and loan capability. It imposed on the limited generosity of friends. Neither one had any close family or relatives to beg from. Eric sold their old car for what few dollars "auction" said it was worth. He sold precious textbooks for pennies on the dollar from their original costs. His dad and mom had left him nothing but the crumbling family house on Flint's old North Side, but the market value of that was virtually nothing. And Eric and Mary still needed some place to live. They couldn't afford even rent on a place that didn't sublet to rats and cockroaches.

At least his mother, Florence, had managed to pay off the small mortgage on the family home before she passed. By the time Mary's funeral expenses were satisfied, you could pick up the rather diminutive Eric by his ankles and shake him upside down until his pockets were empty. But no coins would roll out. Only lint and dust.

And that was Eric's need for cash to help in his "transition" when he took the retirement payout from a downsizing General Motors in late 2008. Eight years after Mary's death, he was still buried by hospital, doctor, clinic, hospice, lab, radiology, oncology, virtually every bill ever conceived of by the American Medical Association (AMA), American Hospital Association (AHA), and countless other medically related agencies and offices. The payout money wasn't sufficient to settle everything, but after that resource was wiped out, at least the mountain was bulldozed down to a collection of monthly payments that he could possibly handle.

But he had to go back to work. Not as a college professor or teacher, but at what he could find at almost sixty, a janitorial job at a North Side elementary school that he could reach by walking, however unsteadily, and a short bus ride. His compulsively positive and upbeat spirit had undergone severe strain and testing. But he had to keep determined. He couldn't let anything, or anyone, defeat him. "Happy thoughts in your head and a smile on your face," had been Momma's dying words. They defined Eric Darden.

CHAPTER FIVE
A Life of Loss and Continual Harassment

Eric Darden suffered catastrophic losses throughout his life. Such hardship would challenge anyone His abused childhood was one unrelenting loss. Loss of safety. Loss of nurture and support from his father, Dante. Loss of his dad's life. First in prison. then in death. He lost his siblings when they were kicked out of the family home and forced to find their own way. He lost his beloved mother and anchor in his life when she died in 1989. And he lost his soulmate and perfect life partner in 2000. He in effect lost his college professorship in 2008 when GM shed the old GMI and handed off to Kettering. He lost all financial resources. Including the retirement package buyout. He lost his car. His most precious things. His books. He lost everything others would consider to be an asset of value.

That one exception was the old, ramshackle family house. It needed upkeep and repairs that he couldn't afford to make. In fact, it might have been seized and torn down through eminent domain by the City of Flint had it not been for the fact that there were just too many such houses in the city for the municipal authorities to deal with. Once General Motors, the largest employer by far, pulled out and abandoned Flint, there were hundreds. The entire city and its essential infrastructure – such as the infamous water mains and pipes crisis – posed far larger and more pressing crises than the Darden family house.

In fact, the houses on each side of Eric's house were in even worse shape. They had holes in roofs. Every window broken by vandals. Graffiti spray-painted on every side. Crumbling, hazardous sidewalks. Collapsing porches. Interiors occupied by a variety of animals and druggies. It was no wonder that Eric's house had no reasonable market value. The location was horrible. The college professor turned janitor had by all measures lost his immediate neighborhood as well.

In some respects, Eric's losses were even greater – if that could possibly be – in his personhood, his core identity as a man, as a human being. The phenomenon of "living while black" affected him from early childhood. When he was a preschooler, a group of children playing in a North Side park had swung the seat of a playground swing so hard at Eric's face that when he managed to duck the metal seat, it swung back and broke one of the brats' nose, blooding it. When parents and guardians rushed to find out what all of the crying and hollering was about, the three white kids chorused that "It was the n.....r kid's fault." A park security guard banned Eric and his mom from the park. "And you're lucky I don't call the police and have him taken away from you."

The police did get called one day when young Eric was walking home from Potter Elementary School. He was followed closely by three older students, all three white in those days when there was more racial diversity. Once out of sight of the school and other kids, they caught up to him on the sidewalk. They grabbed him and proceeded to punch and kick him, including as he lay covering his head and curled up trying to protect his belly and crotch. One kid rifled through his pockets as the other two continued the assault. His few coins for lunches the rest of the week were taken. A neighbor looking out at the street called the cops. "There's a bunch of kids fighting out here. One of them is a darkie."

When the patrol car arrived with its arrowhead shield and motto on its door, "To Protect and Serve," the two officers could only grab one of the young toughs while the other two ran off. "My buddies and me were only defending ourselves," the kid claimed. "This Negro kid was trying to take our lunch money. That's his jackknife on the ground over there." The white kid was sent home. A pained and bleeding Eric was taken to the North Side Flint Police "Mini" Station. He was held in a holding cell on suspicion of attempted theft and assault with a deadly weapon. It was a serious charge that ended up costing him juvenile court time, a period of probation, and restrictions on his activities before and after school.

Eric's father had been furious. He refused to retrieve Eric from the police station. Flo had to do it. But his father's swinging belt awaited him when he got home. Both the physical and the psychological beating hurt worse than what he suffered from the delinquents. It was not the last time Eric had a bad experience at the hands of the police sworn to protect and serve.

As grade school transitioned into middle school, middle school into high school, Eric went through a countless number of incidents of being stopped and frisked for walking home while black. Standing on a street corner while black. Riding a bus while black. Looking for things to buy in a corner store several blocks from his house while black. He learned to live and breathe under a cloud on constant suspicion. He was on different occasions accused and even arrested for things he didn't do, would never do, and didn't even think of doing.

Eric's loss of independent personhood and manhood was perpetual. As the only black student at GMI, he was concluded to be there only as the original "Affirmative Action" enrollee. Flint police around the institute repeatedly stopped him and questioned what he was doing there, why he didn't go back to "his 'hood,'" and hands on the hood of the patrol car while they checked his ridiculous claims of being an enrolled student on campus.

At Michigan State University he was a puzzle for many. Why would a short, small, young black man be enrolled in graduate school there? His size and his constant limp ruled him out as a student on athletic scholarship. Was the stack of books under his arm or in his backpack for show? More than once, Eric had been assumed to be one of the custodial staff, a food service employee, or an intruder from off campus. East Lansing and University Police picked up the job of stopping him, sometimes retaining him, from their colleagues on the Flint City force. It was a deeply ingrained part of the police culture.

One time he was arrested for walking while black past the fringes of an Anti-Vietnam War Protest. It had been assumed that he must have been one of those who tossed a brick at security and police cordons. He was finally released when there was no evidence that he had done anything violent, but he was issued a stern warning anyway.

Even as a professor at GMI Eric experienced the lifelong loss of dignity and freedom. As the first and only black faculty member, he again was assumed to be custodial, or a service employee, or someone who obviously didn't belong there. The Flint police ignorantly picked up the police "baton" that had once been handed off to East Lansing and back again. Professor Darden resumed being stopped and detained while doing whatever he was doing black.

It was something of a wonder that he didn't go over to the constant feeling of *rage* written about so eloquently by James Baldwin. The armed "copwatching" and resistance of Huey Newton and Bobby Seale's Black Panthers in the late '60's would have had logical appeal. Malcom X's strident calls for black empowerment and the separation of black and white Americans could have appealed to his lifelong sense of loss and oppression.

But none of it was Eric's way. Jesus Christ's "turn the other cheek," pray for those who persecute you, and do not return evil for evil, held sway for him. He resonated to Leo Tolstoy's pacifism, Mahatma Ghandi's nonviolent resistance, and Martin Luther King, Jr.'s nonviolent civil disobedience. It did not escape his notice that three out of the four great men had been assassinated or executed.

But more than anything else, it was his momma. Among her many teachings to him and her words to live by was her fervent belief that God's justice would ultimately prevail. "Stay the course, Eric, my son." And so he did, despite the loss of virtually everything. And it was not over.

CHAPTER SIX
Eric Darden's Backyard Beehive

Eric would have liked a dog. His family had acquired a puppy when he was in grade school. His dad, however, couldn't tolerate the puppy's natural playfulness and noise. It was a good-natured dog, eager to please, but it wasn't in the house one day when Eric came home from school.

"Where's Sparky?" Eric asked when he came in and set his books down.

Dante belched, then took another deep swig from his beer bottle. "Noisy little beast got poisoned by someone with chicken bones." He moved back to watching his television.

That loss was also devastating to Eric. Sparky was such a pleasant little mutt. It was common in Eric's childhood to explain a dog's death by poisoning from being fed chicken bones. To what extent that actually happened was highly debatable. The theory was that fragments of splintery chicken bones could lodge in a dog's throat, stomach, intestines, and end up killing it. Truth of the matter, Eric had never known of that actually happening. There was no replacement dog, or any other kind of pet.

It was not until some time after Mary's death and burial that Eric found a living replacement for a pet. He acquired a hive of calm, easy to tend, Italian honeybees. He set the white hive box up in a back corner of his backyard. At first it was just a classic, cube-shaped box with rows of hanging wax comb frames inside. It was painted the usual white, with an aluminum covered lid to reflect back the hot summer sun's rays and shed the rain. The design featured an open slot at the bottom of the front of the hive which provided entrance and exit for the bees. There was also a narrow "porch" strip that bees could land on coming in or launch from flying out. The hive box sat on two construction cinder blocks that Eric had retrieved from a nearby house demolition. That kept the hive off of the ground, out of wet puddles in a rain. It also prevented easy intrusion by ground-crawling invaders like ants or bumblebees.

All in all, the classic beehive design and construction was simple, but ingenious. And the starter colony of honeybees Eric introduced to it settled right in like "at last, home, sweet home." Acquiring the starter colony was an interesting experience for Eric. True to his nature, he researched and readily found several professional apiaries in more southern states that routinely sold and shipped "packages" of starter colony bees, especially the all-important, egg-laying queen.

A box of bees consisted of a wire mesh cage formed around a wooden framework in a rectangular shape. Inside the box would be roughly 4-5000 bees split off from an established, productive colony down south. Dangling in her own special "queen cage," sealed on one end by a simple cork, would be her highness, the queen. Queens were only one to a colony, and a queen shipped within a box of bees had to be checked and verified to be actively laying eggs and producing new bee larvae before she would be sold and shipped with the box to start a new colony.

Contrary to colloquial references to a woman as a "queen bee" in some social group or clique, actual queen bees are not ruling monarchs over 50-60,000 worker bees. They are more like pampered slaves. Their sole function is to lay eggs and produce more young bees. The colony as a whole is totally devoted to their queen. They defend her with their own lives. Attendant bees feed her and groom her, picking off any parasitic little lice that may try to latch on. But she is expected to be an egg laying machine. Her attendants will encourage her in her all-important work. They will prod her if she's not diligent. And they will start feeding a new queen larva to replace her when she ages and can no longer keep up.

The colony depends upon their queen for its existence. In the height of the spring-summer blossoming season, another colloquial saying comes directly from the bee colonies – "Busy as a bee." A worker or foraging bee, always an infertile female, will gather nectar for honey or pollen for protein for perhaps a total of six weeks. By then it has literally worked itself to death. Filmy wings tattered, it expires – whether somewhere out in the foraging fields or at home in the hive. If in the hive, its carcass will be unceremoniously hauled out by "house-cleaning," undertaker bees and dumped overboard from the little front porch. Foraging ants and other scavengers make quick work of removing it. But it has to be replaced, since hundreds can die each day. So, the queen better keep laying, especially if the colony is growing and may split off a swarm to start another, new colony somewhere else.

Each colony of bees is completely attached to *their* queen. They all came from her originally. They can identify her by her unique pheromones or smell. They do not ever want to be separated from her smell and that of their colony as a whole, except when they have to be out foraging for nectar or pollen.

The exact kind, or strain, of honeybees within a particular colony depends solely upon the nature of the fertilized eggs that queen is laying. Eric had prudently ordered "Our mildest, easiest to work with, productive Italian strain honeybees." Packages of honeybees are typically shipped via the United State Postal Service. Post offices are obligated to receive, ship, and briefly hold such packages of bees. Eric had never in his life, as a private citizen or a college professor, ever gotten such prompt and urgent service from his local post office. A postal employee called him immediately and said over the phone,

"We have wire box of bees addressed to Eric Darden. Are you actually expecting this shipment?"

Eric smiled delightedly, "Why yes, I am." Before he could say anything else, the postal lady raised her voice noticeably.

"Well. Come and GET THEM! NOW!" There would be no home delivery. Not by his carrier, no sir.

Eric had to take an early lunch break from his janitorial duties at the school to go pick up his bees. When he arrived at the branch post office and inquired at the counter, the person on duty brusquely told him, "Janice will take you back to the loading dock." He followed the woman with the name tag, "Janice." Back on a table against a side wall was the package of bees. Janice was not about to go any closer than she had to but pointed.

"There. That's it. Please remove them. They're already starting to escape."

Eric could see even from a distance that perhaps three or four bees were clinging, occasionally moving, on the outside of the package. *Remarkable,* he thought. *The apiary worker poured the few thousand bees into this little shipping cage. Then he hung the little queen cage from the top opening down into the middle of the mass of bees. A few bees missed being "poured in." And now they have clung to the outside all of the distance from the Peach State to Flint, Michigan, refusing to be separated from their colony and their queen. Just remarkable.*

Janice was already starting to scurry away, back toward the front counter.

"Please take them out that side door from the loading dock area to the drive and parking lot. Do NOT follow me anymore." She disappeared from sight.

Although lacking personal experience, Eric had researched and studied enough to appreciate that honeybees are very focused on what they need to do. Those clinging bees absolutely needed to stick with the others. Foraging bees need to visit enough blossoms to fill their back leg pollen sacks with the precious pollen. Bees sipping nectar need to fill their stomachs with what will eventually be processed into honey. Each will ignore a person standing right next to them, even leaning over them. Their focus is hard-wired. The stings that concern every person come only to defend, whether the individual bee, or their whole colony.

That day Eric walked the package of bees the several blocks to his house and yard from the small post office. He had to limp slowly, the cage of bees in his right hand, held by a handle at the top of the box. In his left hand he maneuvered the cane he needed to steady his damaged foot. He went down the old side walkway to his backyard. He had carefully placed the new hive box in a corner near the old wooden fence surrounding the backyard. The hive entrance faced the southeast. The rising, warming sun would shine on the slot entrance and "porch," warming the bees from the chill of the previous night. That same area would be opposite the setting sun, so that the hot afternoon sun did not bake the bees going and coming.

Eric set the package of bees down on a little table next to the hive and in the shade. He knew that they would be okay until he returned in a few hours after his shift at the school. He would clock out; the night janitor would punch in.

When he got off of the afternoon bus and walk home, he headed directly to his backyard. *Yup, still there and okay. And the clingers still clinging, waiting to be able to rejoin the others.* He went in his house and brought out his new pith helmet, the bee head net that fit over the brim of the helmet, and heavy, sting-proof leather gloves that extended up to and tied at his elbows. He wondered if he should have bothered to put on the neck to ankle sting-proof bee coveralls. It wasn't necessary. The little swarm of bees and their queen only wanted to relocate in a new hive location. It was their sole focus at that time. *Free us and our queen, and let us settle in our new home,* he imagined them saying.

So, he did. He opened the top of the new hive and removed a couple of the hanging frames of empty beeswax comb. He unlatched the tight-fitting lid on the bee cage. He carefully removed the dangling queen cage and pried off the little cork sealing the hole through which the queen could enter or exit. He then stuck it firmly between two of the center frames hanging down in the hive box. In addition to the cork, there was a small plug of beeswax filling the hole. Once both were in the new hive, the queen herself would start nibbling from the inside of her temporary prison, and the attendant bees would do the same from the outside. Before very long, she would be free, and egg-laying could recommence.

The queen situated, Eric again opened the lid of the package and gently started pouring the eager bees into their new home. He used a soft "bee brush" to encourage a few bees that seemed confused or disoriented by the whole experience. The clingers quickly rejoined their buddies. And the whole mass spread out, satisfied that their queen was in there with them. Only one bee had been accidentally squashed in the process. Finally, he slowly and carefully replaced the two frames he had removed to enable pouring in the bees. He used that brush to encourage a few to make room and move as the frames were gently lowered back in place. *There. Everybody.* He smiled as he thought. *Welcome home and call if you need anything.*

He left and went back into his house to let everything settle down. He couldn't help but look out his back kitchen window from time to time and try to see if there was bee activity visible. But he forced himself to fix his simple supper, brew his evening coffee, and wait a little bit. As the sun slipped down toward that western horizon, he put on a light jacket and took his after-supper cup of coffee out to a chair next to the small table and the nearby beehive. Eric watched and sipped, and right away it was apparent that a few bees were active at the entrance. That included some "guard bees" that monitored anything approaching the hive entrance. The guards could instantly smell if it was one of their own. They quickly sensed if it was a threat, like an obnoxious bumblebee or a predatory wasp. They would welcome and grant passage in for their comrades. They would vigorously grab and eject any "undesirable," stinging to death if necessary.

Seems like we're underway. Eric smiled and sipped. *It won't take long for the queen to be freed, and then things will really get buzzing.* He chuckled at his own corny joke. *Well, good night bees. I'll check on you again in the morning before I have to catch the bus to go sweep and mop the school.*

So, he did, and smiled more as he saw that foraging bees were already headed out of the hive to search for pollen and nectar sources around their new home. They could smell those, too. In fact, when necessary, the bees might fly a mile or two to an especially desirable flower blooming, zeroing in on the perfume of the blossoms in the breeze. *Remarkable.* He could hardly wait to get home that late afternoon and sit by his beehive.

CHAPTER SEVEN
Eric's Start at Beekeeping

Eric's choice of a colony of bees in his backyard was both perfect and far more therapeutic than he could ever have imagined when he decided to try it as a hobby. He still would have liked to have a dog, but he knew that wasn't possible when he was gone off to work at the school from early in the morning until close to supper time. There was no one at home to let a dog out, feed it during the day, keep companionship with it. It wouldn't work.

The bees, however, required little actual care. He provided a shallow pan of water on the little table for when they might need a drink. But he suspected that songbirds and other insects may have benefited even more than the bees. Despite being manipulated by humans, "kept" and used for their honey production, honeybees actually remained "wild" animals. They almost always provided for themselves.

Several days after he had placed his bees in their new hive, Eric got a call from Cherokee Rose Apiaries.

"Mr. Darden," the lady on the other end said, "I'm just following up on your shipment of new hive box, beekeeping equipment, and most recently, your package of Italian honeybees with fertile queen enclosed. Did all reach you in good order? Did you have any problems with setting up your colony? I assume from your total order that this may be a new venture for you. We're here to help, answer any questions, provide you with what you need for successful beekeeping and honey production."

"Well, thank you for your call," Eric said. "Ah, yes, everything arrived just fine. I got the hive box set up. When the package of bees arrived several days later, I had no problem introducing them to their new home. They settled right in and are even now busily doing their thing. Guard bees on duty. Foragers going and coming. 'Busy as bees' I guess you could say. Thank you so much for your products and service. And especially for the bees. They seem to be as mild-mannered and easy to work with as you had advertised. And I'm enjoying them tremendously."

"Excellent," the lady said. "Now two things before I let you go. First, don't forget next week, when you think they're well situated, to mix up the paste of bee food and mite medicine. Follow the directions, press it into a thin pad, and just lift up the lid of your hive box and set it on top of several of your comb frames. The food will help them with nourishment while they start to pack away their own pollen and nectar. And the medicine will help ward off the parasitic mites that can weaken or even destroy your colony."

"I surely will," Eric agreed. "And the second thing?"

"Well, I noticed that your order didn't include any honey supers, and y'all best have those."

Eric had studied enough to know that the woman was referring to shallower hive boxes that a beekeeper would stack on top of the main brood box. A screen called a "queen excluder" was set on top of the main hive box, and the first honey "super" set on top of that. Then the lid replaced. That way, the queen would be confined to the brood box and not creep upward to lay eggs in the empty combs in the super. The nurse bees would also pack comb cells with pollen around the maturing brood of larva in the main box, where it was needed to feed the young bees. Only foraging bees could squeeze between the bars of the queen excluder. Thus, they would pack surplus honey in the shallow honey super boxes. It was that honey that the keeper easily harvested for his own use or sale. Honey stored in the main box was reserved for the bees' own need.

"Oh, you're right," Eric said. "I'm just starting out with keeping bees. I'm not really planning on a lot of honey production. Don't even have jars to put it in."

"You might be surprised," the lady said with cheerfulness and a bit of admonition. "Do you have any fruit trees nearby? Any home gardens, either flower or vegetable? Any vacant fields with lots of wildflowers?"

"Ah, well, now that you ask, I do. All of that, actually. Neighbor in the next block has his own little grove of four plum trees. Shares his plums with me every late summer, early fall."

"You better get at least two of the honey super boxes. And a plan and means to be able to harvest and bottle your honey. Even if you weren't counting on that, these bees are hardworking and very productive. If they don't have the additional hive box capacity to store their surplus honey, they'll find places to put it where you don't want it, sugar. Believe me."

As much as he had learned already, Eric clearly had a good deal more to learn about keeping bees. He ordered during that phone call the two supers, the queen excluder, and two boxes of one pound honey jars, the lids, and blank labels that he could mark when bottling.

"And, we make no guarantees, but you might just tell that neighbor to be prepared for a bumper crop of plums this season. Maybe some jelly jars to make yourself homemade plum jelly and jam?"

The thought crossed Eric's mind *This woman is an exceptionally good salesperson. Do I really need all of this?* But it all came to pass just as she said it would. The plums were great! The honey? Delicious!

CHAPTER EIGHT
Eric's Refuge

Sir William Osler, one of the four founding professors of Johns Hopkins Hospital, is quoted as saying, "The doctor who treats himself has a fool for a patient." As a professor of psychology, Eric Darden knew that it was foolish to try to treat his own mental disorders. But at the same time, he was self-aware enough to know that he was afflicted his entire life by post-traumatic stress disorder (PTSD). The disorder had started with child abuse by his father from an early age.

The disorder had intensified from early kindergarten and grade school in all of those incidents and injustices involved in living "while black." Pain of every type – mental, physical, psychological, spiritual – accompanied the PTSD in every breath he took, every beat of his heart. His dreams and waking thoughts swam in a sea of distress. From his mother's determined teaching to his studies in psychology, Eric suppressed those feelings and thoughts with almost super-human effort.

A common symptom of PTSD is for the person with the disorder to have intensified core feelings of "fight or flight." Since it was totally against Eric's nature to turn in the direction of "fight," whether consciously or sub-consciously he chose "flight."

In whatever way he could, he avoided situations that called up his core trauma. If he could not physically avoid a humiliating, unjust, belittling situation, he mentally avoided it to the extent he could by avoiding dealing with it directly. A smile instead of a comeback. A walk away instead of a confrontation. A change in his daily patterns instead of pushing through it. A "turn the other cheek" instead of a counterblow. An insistence on love instead of an act of hate.

Eric knew that his mental disorder needed treatment in counseling/psychotherapy, probably medication with which he was well familiar. But like untold millions of people with mental disorders, he convinced himself that "he could handle it." He was a professor of psychology, after all. He knew what to do for himself. Without ever thinking about it in those classic terms, he had a fool for a patient.

But the bees surprised him. As days passed into weeks that spring and summer, he found that simply quietly, peacefully, sitting and watching the activities of the bees was somehow calming and therapeutic. His backyard hive, table, chair, and ever-present cup of coffee became his refuge. He never tired of watching the lives and work of his bees.

Eric admired their total focus on what needed to be done. He saw order, incredible organization, in their assigned roles and duties. *How does a bee know that it's supposed to be a guard bee, or a nurse, or a cleaner of the hive, or a foraging worker seemingly content to work itself literally to death in its gathering? How does it know that its primary function is to care for the all-important queen, feeding her, grooming her, encouraging her in her laying, prodding her to be more productive? How does a mass of thousands of them know they have to split off into a swarm to start a new colony in another location, another hive? How do they decide who goes and who stays with the original colony, to continue its existence?*

There were so many questions and mysteries in the secrets of the bees. It was *remarkable*. He had a colleague at GMI who lived outside of Flint on a small "hobby" farm. He had a small flock of sheep among his farm animals. Learning some facts about bees from his area farmers, he was convinced that honeybees were more intelligent than his sheep, which were more than "dumb before their shearer." *That surely must not be so,* Eric thought, *but what intelligence must be contained in those tiny bee brains! It must somehow be a collective intelligence. They actually make decisions about what has to be done at any particular time. They react to changing circumstances. They cooperate to save each other, their queen, their colony, even at the sacrifice of themselves. And if for some reason they lose the all-important queen, they immediately do what they have to do to produce a new queen. The colony must continue.*

Great weights of pain, trauma, injustice, humiliation, and loss – the terrible personal history of loss and loss and loss – seemed to be eased in being with the bees. Certainly not eliminated. Not totally healed by any stretch. But at least set aside. Soothed. Lightened in some deeply felt way. Eric may have had a fool for a patient, but in the backyard refuge the fool felt better. His smile was more genuine, more heartfelt, less put on as a mask of bravado.

I lift my cup to you, little bees, he gestured. The bees paid no attention. They were too busy doing what had to be done.

CHAPTER NINE
The North Side Viking Raiders

The North Side Viking Raiders were a motley collection of mostly street gang wannabes. Their constantly shifting membership was comprised of about two dozen misfits. Their gang leader was a thirty-year-old wannabe himself, Joshua "Jungle" McCarthy, who was something of a dropout from a hardcore biker gang based in the Detroit area. "Jungle" was one of the few of the Viking Raiders who owned a badass Harley. Most of the raiders couldn't afford good quality "hogs."

Not a biker gang, the Viking Raiders were also neither a drug cartel-related narcotic pushing gang, nor a dominating protection racket gang. While they had sketchy girl friends who hung around the gang, neither were they seriously into pimping for prostitutes, nor laundering illegal funds kind of gang. They lacked both the focus and the organization to carry out any of those common street gang possibilities.

As is so often the case, they reflected the characteristics of their leader. They put on the appearance of a serious street gang. They had a fierce looking Viking with a bloody battle ax as their logo and shoulder patch. They like the black leather jackets and vests (especially for those who couldn't afford the jacket). They liked the swagger, the drinking to excess, the loud, obnoxious behavior, the aggressive posturing. Like "Jungle" they boasted of what they could do. About big deals and a gang empire. But actual results were seldom and small. Some of them actually spent time ripping off kids on the way to school for their lunch money, as though they considered that big time thievery.

Ranging in age from late teens to late twenties, the raiders were comprised of high school dropouts, kids who had been expelled from their family homes at turning eighteen, jobless – although some actually did have semi-regular jobs – social misfits. They liked to project a public image of knife-wielding, chain-swinging, "fight you at the drop of a Viking helmet," but most of them really preferred the flight instead of fight response to trouble.

Ethnically, they were mostly of various European and Latino heritage. With his last name, "Jungle" McCarthy liked to boast of old Irish mob roots and connections. There was never any real evidence of that, however. There was generally an animosity toward the majority population on the North Side with its African American identity, but any pretense of being a "white supremacist" or Proud Boys type of organization was also false and overblown. The raiders were racist, but not very prominent in that either.

Motley, mostly nondescript, neither this nor that, wannabes, summed it up fairly well. Despite claiming otherwise, the Viking Raiders had never been in a "gang war." They avoided altercations with other Flint area gangs. They steered well clear of the real drug cartel-related gang activity. About the only open conflicts they engaged in were the occasional bar fights and acting tough and defiant for the Flint Police officers on patrol. Every one of the raiders had some sort of minor misdemeanor, some petty crime, some juvenile record at least, in police files. But even the Flint Police couldn't really take them all that seriously. The police would have treated them a good deal differently if they had been a black gang. But they weren't. One raider even had a cop for a mom. He went home to his parents every night. They regarded the Viking Raiders as very minor league, a relatively harmless phase for their immature son.

The rip-off money the gang members took in went mostly to booze, pizza, and a little grass to smoke. To save on "hangout" expense like rent, for a few years now they had squatted in the first couple of floors of the abandoned McLaren office building in their supposed "territory." Normally they would have been evicted and routed out, but the McLaren Corp. had washed its hands of the building and real estate when they reduced holdings in Flint. The city and police force would have cleared them out, but there were so many vacant buildings, abandoned properties, and vacant lots from demolished home and other buildings, that funds to deal with the matter were severely lacking. So long as a serious safety crisis didn't exist, or a public health threat, well, authorities would get around to it...eventually. And even safety hazard or public health threat might well be ignored.

Lacking any marijuana, the rare packets of coke, or some pilfered uppers and downers to hustle, and looking for something to do, Lance Jones and Steven "Skater" Kelly decided one day to pick on some of the most vulnerable of their occasional targets – strong-arming grade school kids for lunch money or spending money. Not that it would have concerned Lance and Skater anyway, but one of the features of such despicable predation was that almost always their young victims were too embarrassed to tell parents or teachers what had happened. Or they actually bragged about it to buddies. "Yeah, I got rolled by two big Viking Raiders for my money, but I wasn't afraid. They ran off right away."

Skater and Lance were on their way early to catch kids a block or two before they reached the school when they saw Eric limping along with his cane and his lunch bucket. Eric had just gotten off the bus a block away from the school and was headed to clock in. Lance and Skater recognized a new target of opportunity.

Eric represented a lot of what the two "toughs" hated and resented. He was black. He was old and feeble. He was small and surely a weakling. And he was gimpy. It didn't take long for them to dub him, "old gimpy-limpy."

They followed close behind him, and when he reached the corner where school property began, they pounced like the pitiable predators they were.

CHAPTER TEN
The Assault

Stepping up close behind an unsuspecting Eric, Lance kicked Eric's cane so hard that it flew out of his hand and into the gutter of the street. Eric meanwhile lost his balance and fell heavily to the sidewalk. He struck his head on the concrete, causing a gash to his forehead. As he lay there, stunned, Lance proceeded to give him a couple of sharp kicks to his ribs. Meanwhile, Skater retrieved the cane and joined in. He gave Eric a couple of blows to his bleeding head with the cane.

Practically unconscious, Eric had a sense that the two tough guys were rifling through his pockets. They easily found his wallet and an old change purse. Lance and Skater took all of the cash, $43 in bills, 66 cents in coins. They also took a couple of credit cards. Although they had no idea who she was, just to be mean they removed a photo of Mary and tore it in two. The only other thing of value was Eric's bus pass. The two ignored that, although later it occurred to them that if they had taken it, at least one of them could have ridden the bus and pickpocketed or otherwise swiped things from unwary passengers.

They left Eric and his cane and lunch bucket on the sidewalk. But before they took off, Lance had the presence of mind to check the contents of the bucket. He claimed the sandwich inside for himself and gave the apple and banana to Skater. Lance wasn't all that big on fruits and vegetables. In a parting show of contempt, Lance swung the lunch bucket at Eric's head, delivering another ringing blow.

"See ya around, gimpy-limpy," He sneered at the curled-up Eric.

"And you can count on *that*," Skater added ominously.

Then, just in case any witness had observed the incident and called the police, Skater picked up his skateboard and pushed off quickly down the street toward their headquarters. Lance trotted along with his old sprinter's powerful stride. After a couple of blocks, the two figured they were in the clear, and they slowed down to chuckle about how easy that was.

"Job well done," Lance chortled.

"And more profitable than ripping off those school kids," said Skater. "I wish he would have had more, but we got enough for a cheap bottle of vodka, a twelve pack of beer, and some smokes. We may even share with a few of the guys."

"Plus," Lance said, "we may have stumbled on a gift that keeps on giving. We know that gimpy-limpy takes the city bus, gets off before school opens in the morning, hobbles down a couple of blocks to get there. He has to be doing the reverse after school lets out in the afternoon. Let's do a little more surveillance and figure out where he lives. A soft target like that, we can get him either coming or going on each end of his pattern."

CHAPTER ELEVEN
After the Assault

A group of four sixth graders came along shortly after Skater and Lance had taken off. They saw Eric still curled up on the sidewalk, holding his injured sides, bleeding from his head, and moaning painfully as he tried to breathe. He was semi-conscious at best, likely suffering a concussion at the least.

"You okay?" one of the kids asked. All of them could see that he wasn't. They hustled on into the school. One of them saw the Vice-Principle and said, "There might be something wrong with that old janitor guy, the one with the limp. He's just lying on the walk down at the corner."

Vice-Principal Simmons handed his check-in sheet to his assistant, called for the night janitor who was just about to clock out and go home, and the two went out to investigate. They found Eric as the kids had reported.

"Eric, what happened?" Simmons asked anxiously.

"M-mugging," Eric wheezed painfully.

Simmons and the night janitor clumsily and briefly debated whether it would be best to call right then for police and an ambulance, or try to take him to the nearest emergency room themselves, or...

"Nurse," Eric managed to get out. "Help me get into our nurse, please."

The school was large enough to have a school nurse on duty while the children were in classes. She had her own office and basic first-aid supplies. She was not authorized to administer any medications other than a few things like aspirins for headaches. It was strongly communicated to all schoolkids and their families that she definitely *did not* have uppers, downers, anything even similar to narcotics. It was, however, a closely guarded secret that she *did* have a supply of birth control pills and things for menstrual relief. Those items were kept under lock and key, but they were there in recognition of the realities of modern times.

The nurse made Eric as comfortable as possible on a small folding cot at one side wall of her office. She cleaned up his still bleeding head and administered at least temporary bandages. She used a small flashlight and checked for signs of concussion. She gently touched his ribs and received a painful jerk and moan in return.

"It's pretty certain that you suffered both a concussion and seriously injured ribs, Mr. Darden. They could actually be broken, or at least deeply bruised. I need to call for the ambulance and paramedics. I'll also have to fill out the standard incident report."

The initial pain and shock at least subsiding, Eric pushed through the waves of pain and teetering consciousness and was able to speak somewhat louder and more clearly.

"No, no ambulance. I'm sure that it's not really as bad as it looks. I know you have to complete the incident report. Put down 'patient refused treatment' if you must. I'll call the police myself. But I really just want to get home. Rest. Get my head together."

He turned to Vice-Principal Simmons. "Jerry, if you could give me a sick day, maybe for tomorrow, too? And if someone could give me a ride to my house, I'd be most grateful. I don't think I can negotiate the walk and the bus right now."

Eric was so definite about what he wanted, and he was so well liked and appreciated by the staff at the school, that against better judgment it was done as he requested. An hour later one of the administrative assistants gave him that ride home and helped him into his house. His cane and his lunch bucket had been retrieved and taken along with him.

He insisted that he would be okay, so the administrative assistant drove back to the school after getting Eric as comfortable as possible in a living room easy chair. Before he settled in, he got some pain pills out of a kitchen cupboard. That gave Eric a brief moment to look out in the backyard in the direction of the beehive. He would really have preferred to be out there, having a healing therapy session with his bees, but he knew he couldn't manage that effort at the moment. He spotted some coming and going by the foragers, however. Somehow, even just knowing they were there and having a glimpse made him feel at least a smidgen better.

With rest, pain pills on a regular schedule, and carefully wrapping some stretchy athletic tape around his painful torso, he began to feel a little bit better by bedtime. He slept uneasily in the old guest bedroom on the main level of the house. Getting out of bed the next morning wasn't easy. He was stiff, achy, still hurting, and started his second day off with a quick, easy breakfast and the first pain pills of the day.

It was inevitable that some food and some pills helped him to manage better. Before long Eric made it out with his morning coffee to sit by the hive. He watched as usual and was especially excited to see some foragers emerge on the porch and flutter their wings that were noticeably bright and shiny. It was now a little over three weeks since he had introduced his package of bees and their queen to his hive, and the bright, new-looking wings were a clear sign that the queen's egg laying was resulting in young bees to build up the colony. He wondered if he was engaging in wishful thinking, but he convinced himself that there were more worker bees coming and going from the entrance. Indeed, assuming all went well and the queen did her job, his original start with 4-5000 bees would become at least ten times that many by the height of the summer season.

He knew full well that his horrible assault would exacerbate his

PTSD. Some of his dreams during his uneasy night reached back into that long personal history of abuse, loss, physical and mental pain, and crushing life experiences. But as he had come to rely upon, the bee therapy helped. It took him into a world where order, harmony, and peaceful existence prevailed. It certainly didn't heal or cure him of all of the suffering, including yesterday's assault, but it maintained that positive, hopeful, do not be defeated spirit that he had been taught. That he had chosen for his path in life. He believed that he could stay the course.

CHAPTER TWELVE
A Pattern of Persecution

Eric neither knew, nor could he really anticipate, that his course would continue to include Lance and Skater. The two hoodlums didn't have any ideas or plans to go after Eric on anything like a daily basis. That would be counterproductive. But they meant it when they agreed that he could become one of those "gifts that keep on giving."

In keeping with both the ingrained disorganization and the general sloppiness of the Viking Raiders, the partners in crime didn't follow a strict schedule on anything. There wasn't anything like a weekly system in their preying upon everyone in their territory from schoolkids to purse-snatching to protection money from a few neighborhood merchants to...Eric. They had no regular schedule for hustling those packets of marijuana and poor-quality coke or pills on their preferred street corners and alleys.

Probably the most regular "schedule" they followed was boozing and partying almost every night. All of their illegal money-making activities were more apt to be whatever they felt like that day. That said, they did follow through on their discussion and the next week they made a point of waiting off campus near Eric's school to observe his departure and limping walk to his bus stop. He had felt well enough that Monday to return to work, however painful and uncomfortable it tended to be.

Eric's bus ride wasn't very long, only several blocks, and Lance easily found out what stops that particular numbered bus made once it left the one near the school. In fact, with North Side area traffic, the two actually made it to Eric's stop near his house in time to spot him limping home. They didn't try to catch up to him or do anything criminal at that point, but they had succeeded in their surveillance. They knew his pattern, and the persecution could commence.

Two days later, on a Wednesday, they acted upon their evil intent. They hit Eric after he had exited the bus near his home and after he picked up a few grocery items at the corner store. Eric had to make a determined effort to manage his cane with his left hand while he hefted his grocery bag with handles and his lunch bucket in his right.

When he reached the alley that ran behind the store, Lance and Skater stepped out from behind a set of dumpsters.

"Well," Lance said, "if it isn't old gimpy-limpy. We meet again."

Eric had sincerely hoped that his mugging the previous week was a onetime thing. Despite his promise to do so, he had not reported the crime to the police. His years of having to deal with police in different cities was not an encouraging history. But in case he would encounter the two Viking Raiders again, he had decided upon a psychological ploy of disarming friendliness.

"Gentlemen," he smiled, "how are you this fine day? Our previous meeting was so brief I didn't have the pleasure of introducing myself and learning your names. I'm Eric, and I'm a retired college professor." That last bit he had decided to toss in. There was always a chance, however unlikely, that the hoodlums held some measure of respect for teachers. They did not.

"Cut the crap, gimpy. Let's see what you have in your bag." Lance grabbed it roughly out of Eric's hand, knocking his empty lunch bucket to the cinders as he had the week before. Skater joined him in dumping Eric's grocery items onto the alley. The carton of milk cracked open and made a puddle. They stomped on his loaf of bread and dumped his essential can of coffee to mix with the alley cinders. Other items they tossed or kicked aside.

"What? No whiskey. No smokes. What are you, some damn boy scout? There's nothing here we can use."

Lance gave Eric a fist in his still sore ribs. Eric doubled over and practically fell. He struggled with his cane to maintain his balance.

"I think he remembers our first meeting from last week," Skater snickered. "Want more of that?"

"And we'll give you more if you don't hand over that wallet," Lance added. "And I mean NOW!"

Again, in case there might be a repeat incident, Eric had taken some precautions when he started back to work that previous Monday. He kept only a few singles in his wallet. He wouldn't have had any cash at all, but he had read that if a mugger didn't find at least *something* to take, he was more apt to become frustrated and violent. Eric had also removed credit and debit cards from the wallet. There was his taped together photo of Mary, his photo ID from the Department of Motor Vehicles, his current membership card in AARP, his Medicare card, and a few receipts he wanted to check against bank transaction records. He made a point not to carry Social Security ID card and number. There were a few coins in his old change purse, but in total, very little money. He had taken to hiding a charge card in his shoe.

"What game are you trying to play with us, gimpy?" Lance almost cursed. "This is a waste of our valuable time. What a pathetic loser, you little bastard." He gave Eric another punch in his throbbing rib cage. Skater added a blow to Eric's still bandaged forehead, for good measure. Lance threw Eric's wallet on top of the garbage and debris filling up the dumpster.

Eric almost fully collapsed at the blows, sinking to his left knee while trying to remain upright by balancing with his cane and right leg. He grew light-headed again, having never actually gotten any treatment for the previous week's concussion. In his mental fog he managed to hear Lance growl to his partner.

"Come on, we need to find a more productive mark, and right soon."

The two left quickly, not even bothering to administer more

beating, to toss away Eric's cane, or even to taunt and humiliate him any further. At least this time. They weren't finished with their plan of persecution.

Eric returned to the steps going into the old corner store and sat down to try to regain his thinking, sense of balance, and full consciousness. He sat for several minutes, trying to clear his head and holding his reinjured side. Gradually thoughts coalesced in his stressed mind.

Two run-ins now with the same two thugs formed some definite categories in Eric's thinking. He wasn't a mental disorder diagnostician as a professional psychologist, but it seemed clear to him that he was encountering two cases of serious antisocial personality disorder (APD). It is a disorder characterized by blatant disregard of the rights of others. APD was often expressed in impulsive and aggressive behavior.

He hadn't learned their names, but he suspected that the taller of the two, and presumably the leader, was a psychopath. He displayed no empathy nor moral concern toward Eric. He was easily inclined to violence and might well be narcissistic. The shorter one seemed to follow the other's lead, seconding what the leader was saying or doing. He might have been considered sociopathic, differing from most people in his sense of right and wrong. But Eric knew enough to understand that the lines were indistinct, often overlapping, with psychopaths and sociopaths. Antisocial personality disorder would probably be the category, if the two would ever be examined and diagnosed by a mental health professional. But they wouldn't be.

Eric regretfully admitted to himself that he needed at that point to call the police and report the assaults upon his person, the thefts, and the willful destruction of property. But he didn't have to. At that moment, a Flint Police patrol car pulled up alongside the curb outside the store.

Someone must have witnessed what just happened to me and called the cops. He gathered his thoughts as best he could to make a statement to the two officers.

CHAPTER THIRTEEN
Eric Encounters the Police

Eric had no idea that the two police officers were on the scene not *in his behalf*, but *because of him*. The clerk on duty behind the counter at the little store had looked out and observed Eric sitting on the front steps, slumped and holding his head and side.

"Damn drunks," the clerk muttered, "loitering in front of the store, scaring off customers. Well, I'm calling it in. The police can deal with him."

The two police officers exited their patrol car and approached Eric, who winced but offered a smile. But before he could speak, one of the officers uttered stern commands.

"Sir, remain where you are. Keep your hands visible to us at all times. Slowly place your weapon down in front of you and kick it in my direction." The cop kept his hand on his baton, next to his holstered pistol.

"Weap...weapon?" Eric confusedly stammered. *He must be referring to my cane. It's no weapon.* Nonetheless, he did as he was told. *Something's terribly wrong here.*

"Now, get up slowly and walk in front of me over to our vehicle. When there, place your hands on the hood."

"I'm afraid that's going to be exceedingly difficult for me, officer," Eric said with a continued pained smile. "My balance and walking ability relies a great deal on my cane." But he rose shakily to try his best to comply.

"Dispatch," the second officer spoke into his shoulder-mounted mike, "we have a possible 390 and a 415 here at Pop's Market. Will keep you posted, over."

Eric had more than enough experience over the years with police to know that the 390 meant "drunk," and the 415 "disturbance." Many would say "drunk and disorderly."

"I can assure you, officers, I have not had a drop of alcohol. I can't with my balance and coordination impairment." Eric did his best to maintain a genial and cooperative tone. But he couldn't help but think *And what disturbance or disorderly behavior have I exhibited? I was just sitting there, injured, assaulted and mugged again.*

It was definitely a struggle to walk over to the patrol car without his cane for balance and support. He wobbled and limped, but he managed to make it and put his hands on the hood of the car as instructed.

Yup, certainly looks like a drunken stagger, the second officer thought. The first officer continued to hold Eric's cane and kept close behind the old professor. But before he proceeded to cuff him, Eric asked politely if he could speak.

"Make it brief," the first officer said, still holding his cuffs at the ready.

"The reason I was sitting on the front steps of the store was that I had just been assaulted and mugged by a couple of members of the Viking Raiders. They ambushed me by the alley that runs behind the store. They struck me several times, threw my groceries on the ground, breaking the milk carton, stomping on the loaf of bread. And they threw my wallet into the first dumpster. Please take a look at the scene, and at my bleeding head."

The first officer looked at his partner, jerked his head slightly in the direction of the alley, and said, "Check it out."

While the second officer did so, Eric's guard said to him, "I'm going to have you breathe into our breathalyzer, and we'll see just how much you've had."

His partner was back soon. "Yah, it's as the old guy said. I retrieved his wallet from the dumpster. Landed on top of flattened cardboard or I wouldn't have touched it."

The two officers glanced at the contents of the wallet, including Eric's DOT identification card. There were no small packets of white, powdery substance that might suggest illegal drugs. There were also no dollar bills.

The breathalyzer was used. "Nope, no alcohol at all registers," said the second patrolman.

"Okay," said the first in a firm tone to Eric, "I should write you up for misdemeanor loitering and obstruction of a place of business. But I'll give you a break this time. Here's a written warning. Don't sit here loitering again. Hear me? Now get going." He tossed Eric's cane on the sidewalk near the patrol car.

As the officers drove off to answer an 11-83 call about a traffic accident nearby, Eric managed to get his cane off of the walk and complied with the command to get going. He would have to replace his groceries later. Right now, he needed home, rest, and his bees. *Almost never has it gone well with the police,* he shook his head. *At least I didn't have to be taken to the station and thrown in the holding cell.* That was another place he had been beaten up years ago.

CHAPTER FOURTEEN
The Persecution Continues

Lance Jones undoubtedly would have been diagnosed not only with antisocial personality disorder, but also intermittent explosive disorder (IED). His sudden outbursts of anger ended up being directed toward both people and property. And now his favorite target was Eric Darden.

Back at their headquarters that evening, Skater and he were on their fourth bottle of their cheap Detroit beer when Skater asked his buddy, "So, when are we going to hit ol' gimpy-limpy again?"

"He's obviously taken some precautions since our first meeting," Lance slurred. "We only got a few dollars out of him behind that shtore. I think we need to send him a shtrongly worded message. Let him know like we do with the convenience shtore owners that he needs to be ready to pay 'protection' fees."

"So," Skater replied, "when and how do we do that?"

"We need to hit up more old ladies and their purses tomorrow," Lance said, "Sho, the next afternoon. After lunch, before gimpy gets home after s-school."

As Lance said, on Friday the two went to Eric's house in the early afternoon. They felt tempted to break in and look for things they could sell and convert into cash. They could also vandalize extensively, just for the fun of it. But they noticed the signs and decals Eric had posted, saying, "Protected by...," a well-known home security company. Not knowing exactly what sensors and alarms were involved, they decided to limit their "messaging" activities to the exterior.

The partners in crime didn't worry about any neighbor calling the cops. The two houses on either side were abandoned, and across the street was a large, vacant lot. They used cans of spray paint to graffiti in large letters "N....r" and "Pay up, G-L" on Eric's front door and siding on both sides of the house. They also broke a few downstair windows with chunks of asphalt from the potholes out in the street. No alarm went off, so finally they looked in the backyard.

They discovered the beehive.

"What's that white box sitting in that corner?" Skater asked.

"Don't you ever get out of the city and drive around in the country?" Lance said. "That's a beehive. See the bees flying in and out down at the bottom?"

"Oh, yah. What's he got that for?"

"Bees, honeybees, dimwit," Lance berated Skater, giving him a glancing slap to his head. "Where do you think honey comes from? Duh."

"Oh, yah," Skater said as he moved a bit out of reach of another whack.

"Come on," Lance said. "Let's mess with his beehive a little bit."

"Oh, man, I don't wanta get stung," Skater protested.

"We'll keep a distance," Lance said. "Go over to his little yard shed at the back of the house and see if there's a garden rake."

There was. Skater brought it over to Lance. Lance crept up near the back side of the hive, opposite the entrance slot. From a distance of a few yards, he sprayed a messy blob of red paint on the blank, white side of the hive box, just to mess it up some. Then, he took the long-handled rake and in a few tries, managed to get under the lip of the hive top and flip it off.

The bees liked neither of those actions. The paint smell was noxious and possibly toxic to them. The loss of their hive lid cover exposed the colony, its honeycomb frames, and critically, the sensitive brood cells to the heat and light of the sun overhead. Both guard bees and worker bees started to swarm around, feeling stressed and anxious to repel an unknown threat.

"Come on!" Lance hollered at his buddy. "We gotta get out of here, pronto."

The two dashed off, but not before Skater got a sting to the back of his neck. "Exactly what I said I didn't want," he griped to himself.

After a while, Eric shuffled home from the bus stop and immediately saw the graffiti on his house. "Those bastards," he seethed. *They beat me. They mug me. They harass me. And now, this? My home. The vandalized my home. Enough already.* He thought about getting some paint remover some paint remover from the basement and clean it off while it's still fresh. Then next I'll call a glass repair service to get out here as soon as possible to replace those windowpanes.

They hit the sides of the house, too.

"The bees. My hive," he gasped.

He hobbled as quickly as he could to the backyard and saw what they had done to the hive. There wasn't time to fuss and fume about that attack on his precious bees. He went into the house, donned his protective bee suit, helmet, netting and gloves, and went back to the backyard. First, he replaced the lid to protect the frames, the brood, and the queen and her attendants.

Next, he used his paint thinner/remover to wipe the red smudge off of the back of the hive box. The bees didn't like that smell and toxic fumes, either. They buzzed ominously around his head and body, looking for a target to repel this mysterious threat. He didn't blame them. His bees were mild and easy to be with by nature, but any creature will be stressed and act in defense when seriously threatened. There was no opportunity to swarm and flee, so "fight" was the natural response.

Other than a very faint, pinkish tinge, Eric managed to get the back of the hive gleaming white again. And the replacement of the lid quickly settled the colony back down. He would withdraw, let things subside to normalcy, and get to cleaning up his house.

He made that phone call to the glass repair service and was assured that a truck could be there within an hour, right after the technician finished replacing a windshield for a car in his neighborhood. Eric calmed down and made a simple pb&j sandwich while warming a cup of the morning coffee in his microwave. The nourishment helped, and even more so to look out the kitchen window and see the bees coming and going as usual.

As he munched, he mused. Such a lifelong student, lover of books and discovering new facts and information, he reflected on his commitment to nonviolent resistance. He still believed very much in love triumphing over hate. He wanted to stay the course in turning the other cheek and praying for those who persecuted him. He was definitely not going to allow himself to be defeated or to give in to sick bullying. Among other things, to do so would have been a betrayal to his sainted mother, a disappointment to his beloved wife, Mary. And he believed that both were "looking down" on him, that God would protect him to the degree that he really needed.

At the same time, Eric was a longtime amateur historian. He knew full well that Gandhi and his allies had what limited success they achieved against the oppressive British Empire in the first half of the 20th century for a reason. For all of the Empire's cruelties, there was a moral core that made oppression and violence against the native Indians unacceptable to at least a significant portion of the English.

On the other hand, resistance against Tamerlane's invincible Mongol armies in the 15th century, whether violent to the utmost, or passively nonviolent, made no difference to the peerless warriors on horseback. They still made pyramids of as many as 90,000 skulls of their victims, and towers of human bones as macabre monuments to the futility of resistance of any kind.

Eric feared that if he was right about his two persecutors, the mental disorders and the intermittent explosiveness, nonviolent resistance and standing up to bullies didn't register as more than an encouragement to keep on preying upon him. If you had no empathy, no moral restraint, short of being physically stopped in your behavior, what was to keep you from continuing to persecute? If nothing else, it became a challenge to be the pain that kept on hurting.

Eric wrestled with his own moral problem of whether he had to do something. A genuine tipping point was the senseless attack on his honeybees. He could chance that the two lowlifes would tire and get bored with victimizing Eric himself. He could clean up vandalism. It was annoying and expensive, but it was just property, "stuff." But to victimize his bees was to seek to destroy his therapy, his healing, his hope for balance and peace in his life. *And that's it!* he realized. *They're destroying Hope.* What to do about it was the problem.

CHAPTER FIFTEEN
What To Do About It?

After his sandwich and coffee, Eric was outside the front of his house, scrubbing with the paint remover and strong cleaning agent, when the neighbor down the street who had the several plum trees walked by and stopped.

"Damn thugs," the neighbor, Alex, cursed. "Those the same Viking Raiders that have bothered you before? And who is 'G-L'?"

"Me," Eric sighed. "Stands for 'gimpy-limpy,' their pet name for me."

"You need to get a gun," Alex grumped.

"No, can't do that," Eric said. "Not only do I not like guns, but I couldn't shoot someone even if to save my life. There's got to be another way to handle it."

"Well, suit yourself, but anyone breaks into my house and my life is on the line, they can expect a double-barrel load of buckshot center mass. And that's the gospel truth. Besides, you can't very well depend upon ol' 'Protect and Serve.' They can't be bothered to protect, and they mostly serve themselves and the wealthy folks. Mark my words."

Eric liked Alex. He was a good neighbor, and generous with that plum jelly. But he was also very no-nonsense about just about everything. They waved a casual goodbye and Alex continued his walk.

Eric ran out of good daylight. He would have to finish his clean up on Saturday. Maybe a fresh coat of paint would be needed in the final result. As his momma had always taught him to do, he put a positive spin on the cleanup. He realized that the whole house could use a sprucing up. Cleaning and painting the entire house were beyond his capability. But this could be a start. And if he saved up, maybe later that summer he can get a professional house painter. It would look a whole lot better and maintain property values in the neighborhood. That last thought brought a smile to his face at last. Yes, his house would look better, but the real estate mantra always prevails, "It's all about location, location, location."

His conundrum continued. What could he do to stop the persecution, and now the threat to his bees?

CHAPTER SIXTEEN
Escalation

Eric wasn't about to "pay up." Neither was he about to obtain a gun of any type. Now he wished anew that he had gotten that puppy, especially a good guard dog like a German Shepherd or a Doberman Pinscher. But that last still wasn't a feasible option. For all he knew, based on his years of experience, calling the cops could just as well result in being investigated for what he had done to provoke the criminal behavior. Neighborhood Watch was of no help when you had no immediate neighbors and your plum guy down the street hunkered in with his shotgun. The home security system he figured had kept the thugs out of breaking and entering his house. Well, from entering, at least. But it might just be a matter of time before they figured out a way around, or how to disable it. And always there was the vulnerable beehive. He couldn't reasonably protect it while he was off doing his janitorial work at the school. He couldn't move it inside the house. And he was not about to remove it entirely, not even to relocate it perhaps to Alex's place. It was frankly a second "crutch" to give him support. Conundrum.

Ironically, it was the two hoodlums' escalation that resulted in a totally unexpected resolution. And nobody could have guessed it might happen.

Having scored a couple of purse snatchings from elderly ladies shopping, Lance and Skater were kicking back at headquarters with their latest booze and beer purchase. But Eric was never far back in Lance's mind and obsession.

"Been thinking about our favorite target, gimpy-limpy," he said to Skater.

"Time to rough him up again and squeeze the cash out of him?" Skater said, raising both eyebrows and bottle.

"Well, sure," Lance agreed. "But I'm not at all convinced he's really gotten the message yet. Besides, last time he seemed to have taken precautions and made a point of not carrying much money at all. And notice that he had no credit or debit cards either. No, we need to create the clear understanding that he has to be able to pay up when we rendezvoush with him."

"Ooh, big word, Lance," Skater said and took a long swig. "So, what we gonna do?"

"Let's make another friendly home visit. And this time we'll make our deal more definite, with more consequences for breaking the terms."

"Yah, I like the breaking part," Skater smiled and kept drinking.

The next day it turned out that "Jungle" had a small, fresh supply of pills and some coke cut with baking powder for them to peddle behind the area high school and in an alley off one of the main streets in their territory. That went well enough, although they had to give a slice to Jungle to cover his cost.

But the following day the two returned to Eric's house about the same time they had struck it before, early afternoon. Most mornings were entirely too early for them, unless they had to prey on school kids going to school. And as much as both would have been perfectly glad to encounter one of their favorite punching bags, they definitely didn't want to put Eric out of commission at that point. They wanted him to be educated to his responsibility to be that gift that would keep on giving. The ne'er-do-wells wanted him to be on their protection rounds.

"So, what we going to do this time?" Skater asked as they

approached Eric's house.

"Here's my plan," Lance said. "You recreate your graffiti on his freshly painted door and siding. Say, 'We mean it, G-L, time to pay us.' More 'N....r' would be fine. Also add, 'Renig on the deal and more penalty and interest.'" Lance liked the connection to his racial slur. Plus, he really didn't know how to spell "renege."

While Skater did that, Lance went back to the backyard and once again got the garden rake out of the little tool shed. He noticed, of course, that Eric had immediately cleaned off the hive box and replaced the lid after their last vandalism. The bees were back to doing their assigned tasks. This time Lance approached the hive from its backside as he had before. Using the pronged, stout metal head of the rake to push with, he shoved with all of his might.

The hive tipped over from its supportive cinder blocks onto its side. The lid came off again, and this time several of the honeycomb filled frames slid partway out of the box, off of their rails that they hung from. A couple even ejected completely from the box. The queen, her attendants, and the all-important central brood cells were exposed to the bright sun, its heat, and the afternoon breeze.

There, gimpy-limpy, I bet that will get the message across. Lance dropped the rake and skedaddled as fast as he could go. Eric's mild, easily tended, honeybees recognized the terrible threat to their colony, and Lance himself got three painful stings before he was out of range of the extremely stressed bees.

Lance hollered at Skater as he kicked his sprinter's stride into high gear.

"Get out of here! We have some very angry bees after me."

Skater hadn't quite finished with his graffiti, but that one sting the first time there was enough for him. He picked up his skateboard and pushed off for all he was worth. Even so, it took almost a full block to catch up to the sprinting Lance. That night they would congratulate themselves and celebrate what had to be a successful escalation of their persecution. But Lance *did* note some redness, itchiness, and localized pain associated with the three stings.

Eric got home a bit over three hours later. Initially he felt relieved that there was no further contact with the two thugs. But then he discovered the tipped-over hive. The bees were swarming around in distress. A good number of them were trying to reestablish in their combs, but chaos and destruction hindered them.

He had no choice but to throw on his bee suit, all of his protective garb, and go out to rescue the colony. It was when he wrestled the hive box back upright on its cinder blocks that he checked on the queen and her entourage. With frames clashing together in the tip-over, she had gotten mortally injured, her egg-filled abdomen crushed between wooden frame supports. He knew what had to be done.

First Eric carefully, actually tenderly, picked up the struggling queen between thumb and forefinger of his gloved hand. He knew that there was nothing that could be done to save her. So, he gave her a *coup de grace,* a mortal squeeze, but carefully set her carcass down on the little table by the hive.

He replaced the frames and their precious combs in their proper order, spacing them as they needed to be, making sure that the brood cells were back in their central position. Then, before he replaced the protective lid also, he carefully placed the dead queen on the floor of the box, as near as he could to the brood cells where she would normally be depositing her eggs.

There, her colony will still scent her unique pheromones. They will stay close to her for a few days until her scent fades away. He felt sad. Not only for his own spirit-crushing loss, but for the queen's completely devoted attendants. They would encourage, prod, even push her dead body, but to no avail. Eventually they would be forced to give up. The blow to the colony, getting into the height of the summer blossoming season, would be catastrophic. Disorganization and disarray would upset the whole population of thousands of bees.

Having done what had to be done, setting up the hive as close as he could to how it had been, Eric hustled into his house and sat down in the kitchen to make phone calls. He noted that it was about time for Cherokee Rose Apiaries to close their office for the day, being in the same Eastern Daylight Savings time zone as Flint Michigan. Rather than waste dwindling time trying futilely to reach that same helpful lady, he retrieved the phone number for another apiary he had researched in Texas. It was in the Central Time Zone, and thus an hour behind Michigan. *They should still be open.* Their ads to beekeepers, both professional and amateur like him, claimed "We supply young, verified and productive egg-laying queens for both new and established colonies of honeybees." Bucking Bronco Apiaries also promised express shipping, next day delivery. They were a little pricey in comparison to the place in Georgia, but there was no time to dilly dally. He phoned, the office manager picked up, and he placed his order.

"Thank you, sir, for being a first-time customer," the man said. "It's end of the day here, but we'll get your new queen out to you ASAP tomorrow. You'll have her delivered the next day. Now just to let you know, she may seem just a little bit smaller and darker than your old Italian queen, but we guarantee productive laying and your satisfaction." Eric certainly hoped so at the premium price and express shipping cost, but he thanked the man profusely. He hung up his call and felt a wave of relief. *Maybe two and a half days after my old queen's death I should be able to introduce the new queen. That should be soon enough to avoid bigger problems in the colony. I hope the new queen is as productive and harmonious as the old one was.*

That evening he watched the bees. They were trying to maintain their set and necessary patterns, but it was obvious to him that the perfect harmony and humming efficiency of the hive was thrown off. In more ways than one, everything revolved around a good queen. Eric felt like staying home from work until the post office called, "Get down here, NOW!"

Two days later the call came. It had only taken the initial delivery of his starter package of bees to establish a strict pattern with the USPS. Once again Janice took him back to the loading dock area and pointed from a distance at a thick, ventilated envelope marked with large letters, "LIVE Queen Bee! Fragile. Handle with care! NO Stamping." Eric turned to thank Janice, but she was gone like a shot. No matter. He knew the drill. Pick up his envelope. Leave promptly through the side door out to the employees parking lot. Do Not go back to the main counter and lobby.

As soon as Eric could get back to his house and yard, he again donned his bee suit and helmet and took the new queen out to the hive. As he had done with the original queen, he removed the end cork from the wax-filled opening on one end of the queen cage. *She looks healthy and active,* he thought. *And as advertised, she's just slightly smaller and darker than the old one.* He removed two frames of comb as he had before.

He glanced down at the carcass of the old queen, now shriveling up, and no longer being paid as much attention by the old attendants and others. Nonetheless, he left it there to continue to provide what fading scent it may have still had. The bees themselves would soon perform the undertaking duties, especially if their allegiance shifted to the new queen. As he had before, he carefully wedged the new queen cage between two central combs, with the exposed exit hole facing the center of the hive. It wouldn't take long before the new queen smell would attract the worker bees and they would nibble and help her be released. Eric replaced the frames and the lid and hoped for the best. *The queen is dead. Long live the queen!*

He went back in his house, which he had dutifully scrubbed again to remove the obnoxious graffiti. He wanted to let the colony settle down as much as possible and try to restore that essential harmony and rhythm. That evening he would try his usual routine of sipping coffee and sitting out by the beehive. He felt like only that would restore his own sense of healing, peace and harmony.

But until evening, he continued to think seriously about his persecutors. He had brooded about them and the problem they senselessly inflicted upon him the last couple of days while he anxiously awaited the arrival of the new queen. A good solution continued to avoid him, but he had decided one thing. Under no circumstances could he leave the beehive unguarded at this point. He would not chance a repeat of this last disaster. At the extreme, he would retire again and live off of dumpster diving with the loss of income.

Short of that unreasonable route, he decided to ask for emergency leave of absence from his janitorial duties at the school. He had plenty of saved-up, unused vacation and leave time, so he requested and got a full four weeks off. *That will provide enough time to make sure that the new queen is laying energetically, and for her offspring to begin repopulating the colony.* But he knew that until the new brood started to hatch, the foraging bees would keep working themselves to death in the busy blossoming season, and the bee numbers would slump at least slightly.

A setback to be certain. But if all went well, the colony would revive within a couple of months or so, by late summer at least. But what to do about the two outlaws and their incurable mental disorders? He had to stand up to them. He couldn't allow the pattern of persecution to continue until he was seriously injured, maimed...or dead. They had to be stopped. But neither was a gun or other extreme violence an answer he could live with. What do you do when you turn the other cheek and teeth are knocked out on that side of your mouth, too?

Gandhi's nonviolent resistance had succeeded to the extent that it did, in part, because so many people participated in his demonstrations and protests, that the cruel colonialists grew frustrated. In some cases, they actually exhausted themselves trying to repel the demonstrators. Increasingly they depleted the tolerance of their own people to support such cruelty.

Eric doubted that he could muster such mass support for his own resistance. Close neighbors were sparse, and Alex had already announced his choice of tactics.

CHAPTER SEVENTEEN
Persecution Paused

About the time Eric received his new, replacement queen, Lance and Skater talked about their money raising thievery and specifically about how to get Eric completely on board with his payments for protection. But then a hiccup caught them by surprise. A routine afternoon purse-snatching resulted in both of them being arrested. It was a careless mistake.

Skater had tried one of his common tactics of skateboarding down a sidewalk outside several shops, rolling up behind a little old lady, and grabbing the handle of her purse as he rolled by. What he failed to notice was that the purse strap passed under a buttoned shoulder epaulet on the lady's jacket. His grab practically knocked the poor woman over, but the purse remained attached to her jacket. It was actually Skater that got pulled off of his skateboard, which proceeded to roll on until it crashed into a lamppost.

Lance was nearby and rushed over to try to help Skater steal the purse, but the shaken woman rallied and wasn't about to give it up. She was a feisty Scotch-Irish American and pulled as hard as she could to yank the purse strap out of Skater's off-balance grab. Lance was about to give the elderly woman a punch to stop her resistance when police officers showed up and took down both

Viking Raiders. As the brouhaha took place, two patrol officers had emerged from the coffee shop next to the scene with their beverages and wrapped sandwiches. Lance and Skater were quickly cuffed and taken to the station's booking counter.

The next two weeks involved far more time with holding cell, Assistant District Attorney filing charges, court appearances with a public defender, time in the city jail, and a blizzard of legal and judicial process that the two partners in crime just hated. Their trial or out-of-court settlement would be weeks away yet, but it wasn't until about three weeks passed before Skater and Lance could resume anything like their "normal" activities. They knew that the justice system wasn't done with them by any means, and that they were apt to draw closer scrutiny from the police, but they tried to get back to the way things used to be. No purse snatching, however.

"What about gimpy-limpy?" Skater asked and belched as they swigged.

"Yah," Lance said. "We need to let him know that we haven't forgotten about him." He paused and mused in his fuzzy cloud of alcohol thinking. "I think this is what we'll do. We're going to hit him at his home this time. There's been no money available going to and from his work at the school."

"He obviously cares a lot about his honeybees."

"Go figure," Skater sneered.

Lance continued. "Forget the graffiti and busting windows and stuff. Go right for the precious beehive. Let's knock it over like we did last time. Smash with that rake. He'll rush out to stop us. He'll forget to shut the back door. We'll grab him, rough him up good, and drag him back into the house. Force him to show us where he keeps cash and cards. Then we grab anything we can pawn.."

"We'll grab and go but warn him that he needs to have $50 a week set aside for us. He pays regularly, and we protect him from future incidents, and worse, that he won't like."

"Sounds like a plan," Skater reached over for another bottle. "Tomorrow?"

"Might as well," Lance grinned and guzzled.

CHAPTER EIGHTEEN
The New Queen and Her Bees

By about three and a half weeks after Eric had introduced the new queen to the colony, he began to notice slight changes in the foraging bee population. He watched as usual, relaxing and soaking in the peaceful rhythm and restored harmony of the hive, and he saw that new, freshly hatched worker bees appeared ever so slightly smaller and darker in color than his old bees had. *Makes sense,* he thought, *the bees are transitioning into a population that more closely resembles the queen who laid her eggs.*

That wasn't the only difference he noted, however. When he sat in his usual spot, after a while a few bees would buzz around him, around his head, as if they didn't appreciate his presence that close to the hive. He didn't suffer a sting, but a couple of times bees brushed against his head and neck. It was almost as if they were trying to push him away, get him to leave. So, he did. He moved several yards farther away. He could still sit and watch their activity, but from more of a distance. *Obviously, the new queen's offspring aren't as mild-mannered as my old bees were.*

He wasn't about to let that fact spoil his "bee therapy," but he wondered how they would react if he had to open up the lid. Or what they would do if he moved to harvest the surplus honey as the calendar flipped past Labor Day?

It could have been his imagination, but Eric felt like day by day the foraging bees were showing increasingly smaller, darker bees, and correspondingly fewer and fewer of the old, lighter-colored workers. They were still energetic, hard workers, however, and he could imagine that the honey cells were filling at a steady rate.

All in all, Eric's contentment was reestablished. And it was certainly helped by the fact that the entire four weeks of his vacation leave, his persecutors were strangely absent. *Did they finally get bored with bullying me? Get convicted and sent to Ionia Correctional Facility or some other place?* He preferred not to think of them at all, or why they were leaving him alone at last. But a major reason he had taken the time off was to be able to guard his beehive from the lowlifes. And they didn't come around. *Well, next week I'll have to resume my work schedule. We'll see if this hiatus from harassment holds longer. Or if the Viking Raiders return from raiding elsewhere and resume their dirty deeds.*

He still had the weekend, then Monday back to the school. He'd let the principal know that he would show up as scheduled. The extra time with the bees had been enjoyable, but he would also enjoy seeing the kids who were involved in the school's summer enhancement programs.

CHAPTER NINETEEN
Africanized Bees

What Eric had no way of knowing was that the Bucking Bronco Apiaries some time ago had experienced an intrusion of Africanized bees. The queen they had so eagerly sent him was, in fact, an Africanized queen. Unofficially, the apiary thought that they had the problem under control, and that their old stock of milder Italian honeybees would prevail. The usual Italian male drones would fertilize new queens, and the Africanized strain would be bred out. But that had not been the case with the queen they had rushed to Eric.

Despite a lot of bad press and tabloid-style publicity, the truth of the matter was that Africanized bees were not that much different that the preferred Italian, Carniolan, or Caucasian honeybees. They originally resulted from crossbreeding western honeybees with East African lowland honeybees. Hives of Africanized bees started showing up in Texas in 1990. A chief difference from the preferred bees for honey production was that the Africanized were naturally much more defensive than other varieties. They react to disturbances more aggressively. They were apt to chase a human intruder over a quarter of a mile, repeatedly stinging.

Just how Africanized bees developed such super defensive and aggressive characteristics is open to discussion, but clearly their native habitat in the lowlands of East Africa was a harsher and more demanding environment than Eric's backyard. Buzzing at and mild pestering of a hungry honey badger was not a sufficient deterrent to defend their colonies.

Given their discomfort with Eric sitting close to the hive, and with the Africanized young workers gradually increasing in number, Eric started to suspect that "Africanization" might be the issue. The slightly smaller size and darker color was another possible indicator. He knew enough to know that the wetter and chillier fall weather that would inevitably arrive in central Michigan would not be favorable for the Africanized bees. Depending upon a hotter and drier climate, there was no chance that they would survive the arrival of winter.

Frankly, Eric didn't know if he could wait that long for the Africanized bees to perish in the colder, wetter weather coming. It was still summer. He wondered if he should reconnect with Cherokee Rose Apiaries and order yet another replacement queen? But if he went that route and eliminated the Africanized queen, by the time a new queen repopulates the colony, summer will be about over. It might be better to let nature take its course and start over next spring? He decided to mull it over during the weekend. He could decide what to do with the start of the new week.

But before he could, Lance and Skater showed up Saturday afternoon.

CHAPTER TWENTY
The Showdown

"**O**kay," Lance said, "You go scope out the house and make sure gimpy-limpy is busy in there. I'll get that garden rake we used before, and we'll really destroy that beehive this time."

"You got it," Skater said.

Lance got the rake, and Skater soon was back to meet him near the backside of the hive.

"He's busy washing dishes and cleaning up after his lunch," Skater said. "Right now, not looking out toward the hive."

"Good," Lance grunted. "Here, you grab the rake handle too, and we'll give it such a push that the hive will totally collapse and break apart."

It only took the "thump" on the back of the hive for the bees to respond like lightning. Or better, like an angry storm cloud shooting painful lightning bolts. Africanized bees swarmed out of the hive by the thousands. And not just the guard bees. Practically every bee not out foraging, except the queen and her close attendants.

"Defensive and aggressive" was a definite understatement. "Murderous" was closer to the mark.

They behaved as if to earn the tabloid moniker often applied to them, "Killer Bees."

Within less than a minute, Skater and Lance's faces, necks, hands, wrists, any exposed skin, were full of painful, red, soon blistering, sting marks. And it didn't take more than seconds for bees to crawl up sleeves, pant legs, under their shirts to broaden their targets.

By the time the two hoodlums had dropped the rake and begun running literally for their lives, they were afflicted with hundreds of stings. But running didn't help very much. As fast as the two could still sprint, the swirling storm cloud of angry bees chased them every step of their way. Lance and Skater tried to cover their heads to no avail. They swung arms at the swarming bees as they ran. That was futile. The bees chased them with single-minded purpose and murderous intent from block to block, practically the entire half-mile to the Viking Raiders' headquarters...where Skater and Lance died as soon as they entered.

Eric had finally looked out his back kitchen window just in time to see his two persecutors drop the garden rake and start running. He could see that a swarm of bees was after them. He donned his bee suit, made sure that he was fully protected, and went out to assess the situation. The hive was essentially unaffected, not moved out of its position on the cinder blocks, and undamaged except for a slight mark on the back where the rake had struck it. No graffiti or any other problem so far as he could see.

Since not all of the bees in the colony at that point in the day had engaged in the chase, several agitated bees were still around the hive to buzz at him and let him know that another human intruder was not wanted at this point. He was followed by the defensive bees as he went back to his house, made sure that none followed him in, and shed his protective suit and helmet once inside.

Eric poured himself a cup of his after-lunch coffee and sat down by the window where he could look out and view the hive from a distance. *Well, I guess a few stings discouraged the thugs from whatever plan of persecution they had for today. I can't have a guard dog, but I guess I now have guard bees. Might be even more effective.*

The incident made up his mind about what to do with the Africanized queen and her offspring. He would let them finish out the summer/fall season. He figured that the arrival of cold and wet, eventually freezing, weather would result in Nature taking its course. The colony wouldn't survive through the Michigan winter. Come next spring, he would contact the Cherokee Rose Apiaries and have the nice lady start him over with a new package of bees and fertile queen. *The post office will be so thrilled,* he chuckled.

Eric never saw Lance and Skater again. He wondered if the bee stings had thoroughly discouraged them, and they had shifted to other, softer targets. He never learned their fate. On the Viking Raiders end of things, Jungle and his band of loosely disorganized criminals were totally mystified about what had happened to Lance and Skater. Obviously, they had gotten into some nest of angry bees, hornets, wasps, or who knows? Spiders? Scorpions? The two had never told their motley club members about Eric's beehive. They didn't want the others to take over their easy target.

The Viking Raiders didn't waste any time trying to investigate just what had happened to the two. Their main concern was what to do with the bodies. Too bad about Skater. Even Lance was tolerated, especially when he was sharing the booze and beer. But the last thing Jungle wanted was for a medical examiner, the cops, or any other civil authorities sniffing around, investigating two unusual deaths, poking around their headquarters, curious about Viking Raider "business."

Late that night the corpses of Lance and Skater were rolled up in dirty, old scraps of carpeting torn from abandoned offices in the McLaren building. In a dark alley behind the building their remains were loaded into an unmarked, black van. Two of Jungle's trusted "lieutenants" drove down to a dark and isolated shore where the Flint River flowed into the larger Shiawassee, which itself flowed to its juncture with the Tittabawassee, creating the Saginaw River. Adding some old, iron sash weights, they tossed the carpet-covered bodies into the main current and watched until they sank out of sight. Then the cleanup crew left.

It was not until almost three years later that an early spring angler fishing for spawning, river-run walleyes hooked a deteriorating old Nike sneaker with his deep diving lead-headed jig and brought it up to his boat. The fisherman was sorely disappointed that he had not hooked one of the two more walleyes he needed to fill out his limit. He was disgusted that the old Nike held several rotting remnants of a human foot.

He should have contacted authorities and reported his macabre "find," but, hey, he had two more fish to catch, and who wants the hassle? He *did* shake the sneaker off of his hook, back into the water, and set off to try another spot on the river. He truly did not need to have any more such "hookups."

CHAPTER TWENTY-ONE
Eric at Peace

Eric's decision and plan worked out. He went back to his janitorial work the next week after seeing Lance and Skater run pell-mell away from his beehive and backyard. Freed of their persecution and what to do about them, things settled back into a more comfortable routine for Eric. He watched his bees from more of a distance, especially after their furious upset over the two thugs. His PTSD eased in its effect upon his thoughts, feelings, flashbacks and dreams. He still had his lifelong history of stress, anxiety, abuse and heavy losses, but he bore those with such pillars as his momma's "Don't let them defeat you."

Eric missed having a closer "communion" with his bees, but he waited patiently, and it worked out as he knew it would. The Africanized bees and their queen faded and didn't survive the bitter cold and wet of the late seasons. When practically all of them were dead, he went out to the hive, pulled off the honey supers that did indeed hold cells of surplus honey that was harvestable, and winterized the hive until next spring.

The following spring happened as he planned. Cherokee Rose

Apiaries sent him a new package of "our mildest, easiest to keep, honey-producing Italian bees," and a strong, young, proven fertile queen to start over. It all worked out as before, and before long he had his bee therapy in harmonious peace once again.

It was for the best that Eric had no way of knowing what really happened to Lance and Skater. He assumed logically that a few fierce stings thoroughly discouraged them, and they gave up bothering him. An extremely moral and introspective man, had he realized that his inadvertent hiving of Africanized bees actually resulted in the two thugs' deaths, it would have bothered him. Murder on Eric's part? No. Negligent homicide? Creation of a public hazard? Totally innocent of any wrongdoing? The questions, doubts, and pestering of guilty feelings would have nagged at Eric constantly. But he didn't know. Truthfully, no one did. The Viking Raiders were down two motley members and shrugged off the loss.

But Eric? Eric felt more peace than he could remember for many years.

The End

EPILOGUE

The author wanted to write this novella using a black, retired college professor, the fictional Dr. Eric Darden, as the main character. It should be freely acknowledged, however, that this author is an old, white, Doctor of Theology, and does not write from personal identity as a person trying to live in the USA "while black." While the Rev. Dr. Hall is a lifelong Civil Rights activist, going back to the 1960's, and began his ministry in inner city San Francisco and Pittsburgh, it is one thing to ally with, and advocate for, African American persons of color. It is an entirely different matter to live as one.

As was the case with previous novellas written during "Covid times," *Swarm* deliberately depicted primary characters as seriously affected by several mental disorders and illnesses. First was the characterization of Eric's father as controlled by *alcohol-related disorder* and intermittent explosive disorder (IED).

It's widely known that alcohol-related disorder and alcoholism are extremely common and terribly destructive in American society. According to the 2019 National Survey on Drug Use and Health (NSDUH), approximately 55% of adults aged 18 and over used alcohol over the course of a month. About 30% of men engaged in binge drinking. The toll such behavior and disorder take is astronomical. People who engaged in binge drinking were 70% more likely to visit an emergency room due to alcohol-related problems.

The economic cost of excessive alcohol use was estimated to be some $29 billion, with $179 billion in lost workplace productivity and $28 billion in medical costs. The NSDUH estimated that 14.5 million Americans aged 12 and older suffered from alcohol use disorder (AUD). And according to the Centers for Disease Control and Prevention (CDC), more than 95,000 people die every year due to alcohol-related causes.

Such large numbers can become mind-numbing. *Swarm* expressed just one family's experience with this crisis in the alcoholism of Eric's father and its destructive, eventually fatal, damage done to the family members.

Eric's father, Dante Darden, was also depicted as suffering from *intermittent explosive disorder*. IED is also a widespread mental disorder and destructive force in American society. The Cleveland Clinic estimates that anywhere from one percent to as much as seven percent of Americans will develop IED during their lifetime. That would be from 3.3 million people to as many as over 23 million people. Counting not only the sufferers, but families, friends, coworkers, neighbors, and many others affected, that's a terrible toll on many sectors of society.

Eric's mother was depicted as being inextricably caught up in her husband's AUD and IED. She was an enabler and a victim of his alcohol and his violent outbursts. In so doing, she joined about 43% of the U.S. adult population who have had to deal with alcoholism in their families. Again, a huge number.

Dr. Eric Darden himself developed severe *post traumatic stress disorder* (PTSD) early in his life. Although there were many forces and experiences that contributed to his serious disorder, being one of the family members severely damaged by his father's alcoholism and IED was certainly one of the first problems creating Eric's mental disorder.

Eric's persecutors from the Viking Raiders wannabe gang, Lance Jones and Steven "Skater" Kelly, were depicted as both being afflicted by *antisocial personality disorder* (ASPD), expressed in excessive aggressiveness. Lance was very possibly also IED, and it was suggested that he could have been diagnosed by a mental health professional as a psychopath. Skater was described as likely a sociopath. Both psychopaths and sociopaths are estimated to comprise about one percent of the American population, so between them, the disorders encompass about 6.6 million people, no small number.

The purpose of writing all of the above mental disorders and catastrophic problems into the story of *Swarm* was to highlight the overlooked and terribly neglected prevalence of mental disorders and illness in American society and persons. All of these critical problems only magnify if considered on a global level, affecting the entire human family.

It is only logical and inevitable that a worldwide pandemic like Covid-19 would exacerbate the above mental disorders afflicting human beings. The NSDUH studies cited above, for example, took place in 2019, the year before Covid. From early 2020 to the present, the numbers would have to be higher and more damaging, rising to more than half of the people polled.

Finally, the response on the part of many states in America to this mounting crisis has been severely affected by budget shortfalls and fiscal challenges. Public assistance offices have been closed, as well as mental health clinics, chemical dependency centers, and even job placement offices. Many efforts have been mounted to try to respond with federal aid, grants, various programs, but adequate efforts to meet the mental disorder/illness continue to be a challenge. It is a crisis and a challenge that we neglect or put off only at great and terrible cost to all of us, our One Human Family.

ABOUT THE AUTHOR

The Rev. Dr. David Quincy Hall is a retired Presbyterian pastor living with his beloved wife, the Rev. Maxine, their daughters, son-in-law, grandson, and two dogs in Oceanside, Southern California.

David is a lifelong civil rights activist, environmentalist, and social justice advocate. His first two experiences in pastoral ministry were in the inner-city areas of San Francisco, California and Pittsburgh, Pennsylvania in the 1960's. He has dialogued with and lobbied members of Congress in Washington, D.C. and state legislators and committees regarding these issues.

His parish ministry was with congregations across the country in Pennsylvania, Michigan, Iowa, Wisconsin and California, in diverse settings including metropolitan, inner city, suburban, medium-sized and small cities, small town, rural, and the North Woods.

One of many critical issues the Rev. Dr. Hall has addressed in his life and ministry is the pandemic of mental illness and disorders that affects most of the American and world population. *Cellaring* came out of a burden on his heart and mind for all the persons he's known and ministered to with those afflictions. It is set in the American prairie region in Iowa and Southwestern Wisconsin in which he studied, worked and pastored years ago.

Like his series of murder mystery novels, *Death Most Unholy*, including the paperback books: *Death Comes to the Rector*, *Death Crashes the Wedding*, and *Death Stalks the Forest*, this novella is in that genre, but with a very powerful and pertinent message.

Made in the USA
Middletown, DE
22 December 2022

16895488R00050